# We Belong Together

## A Book About Adoption and Families

**Todd Parr**

Megan Tingley Books

**LITTLE, BROWN AND COMPANY**

New York ❖ Boston

Also by Todd Parr:

The Daddy Book
The Family Book
The Grandma Book
The Grandpa Book
The Mommy Book

A complete list of all Todd's titles and more
information can be found at www.toddparr.com

Little, Brown and Company

Hachette Book Group USA
237 Park Avenue, New York, NY 10017
Visit our Web site at www.lb-kids.com

First Edition: November 2007

ISBN-13: 978-0-316-01668-1
ISBN-10: 0-316-01668-3

10 9 8 7 6 5 4 3 2 1

TWP

Printed in Singapore

# Dedication:

This book is dedicated to all the children in the world that need a home and a family.

# Author's Note:

This book is meant to be read with someone you love. Every family is different, so feel free to change the pronouns in this text to fit your family.

We belong together because . . .

you needed a home

and I had one to share.

Now we are a family.

We belong together because . . .

you needed someone to help you grow healthy and strong,

and I had help to give.

Now we can grow up together.

and we had kisses to give.

# Now we can all hold hands.

# We belong together because . . .

# you needed a friend

and I knew where to find one.

and we had lots to teach you.

Now we can discover new places together.

CHINA

RUSSIA

# We belong together because . . .

## you needed someone to read to you

and we had stories to share.

and we had love to give.

Now, we all have someone
to kiss good night.

There are lots of different ways to make a family. It just takes  love. Share your home, and share your heart.
Love, Todd